DUCT TAPE

BOOK TWO

BOOK 2

REAL STORIES

by Jim and Tim

J-Pooh,
Duct Tape
Again

W9-BAO-468

Pfeifer-Hamilton
Duluth, Minnesota

Pfeifer-Hamilton Publishers
210 West Michigan
Duluth, MN 55802-1908   218-727-0500

Duct Tape Book Two—Real Stories

Printed in the United States of America.
10 9 8 7 6 5 4 3

Manuscript Editor: Tony Dierckins

Text: Jim Berg and Tim Nyberg
Design, illustrations, and photo manipulations: Tim Nyberg
Photographs: Erik Saulitis, Saulitis Photography, Inc., Corel, Photodex®

Library of Congress Cataloging in Publication Data
95-69489

ISBN 1-57025-078-2

We would like to extend special thanks to the folks all across this great land of ours who have shared with us their uses of duct tape. To our families who have once again given us input and helped bear the burden of our duct tape addiction. To the digital masterminds at Adobe who, through the powers of Photoshop™, have enabled us to share our duct taping talents with the people of the world. Maybe if we would put in a few names in bold type like, oh say, **David Letterman, Walter Cronkite,** and **Paul McCartney,** people would read this page just to find out what they had to do with this book—just a thought. To Pfeifer-Hamilton Publishers for giving us this vehicle to further evangelize the greatest adhesive known to humanity. To the radio stations throughout North America that have helped us to spread the "Duct Tape Gospel." To Manco, Inc., manufacturers of Duck® brand tape, for sharing their wealth of duct tape knowledge. To *The Rocky Mountain News* for sharing their readers' duct tape hints. To sponsors of The Duct Tape Guys Tape the World—World Tour who have so generously supported us with their advertising. And to the members of the Academy of Duct Taping Science for nominating us for this award and—oops, wrong thank you note. Anyway, thanks to everyone for everything.

JIM AND TIM'S DO-IT-YOURSELF PERSONALIZED AUTOGRAPH PAGE

To a special:

☐ Dad ☐ Brother ☐ Grandpa ☐ Uncle ☐ Brother-in-law
☐ Mom ☐ Sister ☐ Grandma ☐ Aunt ☐ Sister-in-law
☐ Son ☐ Daughter ☐ Grandson ☐ Granddaughter
☐ Friend ☐ Neighbor ☐ Boss ☐ Coworker ☐ Other

On the occasion of:

☐ Birthday ☐ Christmas ☐ Hanukkah ☐ Labor Day ☐ First Date
☐ Father's Day ☐ Mother's Day ☐ Wedding ☐ First House
☐ St. Patrick's Day ☐ Bar/Bat Mitzvah ☐ Graduation
☐ New Job ☐ Retirement ☐ Anniversary
☐ Silver Anniversary (the Duct Tape Anniversary) ☐ Other

May the Duct Tape be With You!

Jim and Tim

FOREWORD

If you own this book, you probably also own its predecessor, *The Duct Tape Book,* the revolutionary 1994 treatise that answered America's need for a handy guide to using everyone's favorite adhesive. Then you already know about the book's authors, Jim and Tim. The Duct Tape Guys have been quite busy during the past year. Besides countless public appearances, including ground-breaking ceremonies for the expansion of Duct Tape World, Jim and Tim have been crisscrossing the globe, spreading what they call "The Gospel of Duct Tape."

Along the way they've gathered true stories of how other proud Americans use duct tape. They also exhausted countless rolls in their effort to help restore some of the world's most famous artifacts. Part real stories, part travelogue, this book is a testimony to the selfless dedication that these two perhaps misguided heroes exhibit each day.

During their journey, Jim and Tim stumbled across a copy of *Bartlett's Familiar Quotations.* The Duct Tape Guys were appalled to discover what they consider grievous errors and careless interpretations of great things said by great people about a great tape. As a service, they include in this book some of those famous sayings restored to their original forms, at least as Jim and Tim remember them, with all references to duct tape intact.

Many think of the first duct tape book as Jim and Tim's gift to America. Consider this sequel, then, as a tribute to Jim and Tim—the Duct Tape Guys. On behalf of America, thanks guys!

—The Editor

DISCLAIMER BY THE AUTHORS:

Like our first book, *The Duct Tape Book*, this book contains humor. Please don't try any of the hints that seem blatantly stupid, potentially injurious, disrespectful to human or animal life, or outright dangerous. Some of the hints are REAL, especially those attributed to real people. You may want to try some of these, or you may not. (Whatever the case, you do so at your own risk.) Other hints are merely for your entertainment (that is, of course, assuming you find extreme stupidity entertaining).

You are hereby notified that the advertisements in this book are phony. Don't get mad at us if the phone numbers for Trixie's or the Duct Hair Club for Men don't work, they're not supposed to. If you do happen to own a company called Trixie's Duct Tape-O-Suction Emporium or Ductco, please consider our ad as free national advertising for your company.

Naturally, all real brand names are the registered trademarks of their respective owners.

If you have any duct tape stories or hints that you'd like to share, you can contact us through the publisher or over the Internet at ducttape2@aol.com.

—Jim & Tim

REAL STORIES

As we traversed the globe on our Tape the World—World Tour, we made frequent public appearances and stops that often included making time for interviews on local radio stations. Fans of Duct Tape often shared stories of how they use the ultimate power tool to enhance their lives. Some fans of America's favorite adhesive have even contacted us over the Internet. We have collected these stories and present them here for the benefit of duct tape users everywhere.

These pages also include some of the many submissions to the "Discover New Uses of Duck® Tape" contest sponsored in 1993 by Manco, Inc., of Cleveland, Ohio, manufacturers of Duck® brand tape—our tape of choice. It's everything it's quacked up to be! Manco, by the way, is the largest retail supplier of duct tape in the United States. Thanks, Manco!

We added hints and suggestions for adaptations to many of the true stories. We hope that, with this added input, duct tape aficionados across America can increase their repertoire of taping skills and become Duct Tape Pros like us.

Golconda, Illinois' M.M. keeps a strip of duct tape sticky-side out on her washing machine to hold orphaned buttons until she has time to sew them back on.

Heck, M.M., why not save yourself the trouble of sewing? We just rip off those buttons in the first place and use a stylish strip of duct tape to hold our shirts together.

It was the best of tape, it was the best of tape. — **C. Dickens**

In **San Marcos, Texas, L.B.** keeps water from spraying her bathroom by using duct tape to secure her shower curtain to the wall.

OK, L.B., that's a great way to keep the water in, but how do you get out?

E.S. of **Howell, New Jersey,** fashioned a sling out of duct tape and uses it to hold his two-liter bottles securely in the refrigerator.

Great idea, E.S. Don't forget to save those empty bottles—enough bottles and a little duct tape can make a great pontoon boat!

3

C.M. of **Cleburne, Texas,** gathers dust bunnies by wrapping duct tape sticky-side out around a wooden spoon to reach under major appliances and other hard-to-get-to places.

Good one, C.M. We like to wrap small pets—like turtles or gerbils—and send them under the 'fridge or washer. It saves a lot of time on your knees, but remember to put the dogs and cats out first, or you could end up with a bigger mess than you started with.

4

If at first you don't succeed, use duct tape. **— Traditional**

In **Columbia, Maryland, G.S.** keeps a spare ignition key strapped to the car's rear axle housing with duct tape.

Ingenious, G.S., except now everyone knows where to find your spare key.

Indiana State University student **J.B.** reports that one clever group of fraternity members stripped one of their brothers to his skivvies and duct taped him to a tree until he proposed to his girlfriend. He was eventually rescued by his sweetheart, who cut him down before agreeing to become his wife.

5

Thanks for the story, J.B.—Another marriage secured with duct tape!

Editor's Note: Tim used a similar method when he proposed to Jim's sister—he duct taped himself to her leg until she said yes.

All we have to fear is no duct tape. — **F.D.R.**

After mechanics failed to find anything wrong with his car, **L.P.** of **Indianapolis, Indiana,** covered up that annoying "Check Engine" light with a strip of duct tape.

Good job, L.P. Try this one: put a strip over the rearview mirror to stop the annoying flash of headlights coming up behind you at night.

6 **D.K.** of **Michigan's Upper Peninsula** duct tapes his ice-fishing shanty to seal out drafts.

Wrap the whole shack, D.K., and not only will you be the envy of the lake, but the glare off your fish house will help you find it more easily!

Remember that there is nothing stable in human affairs; therefore duct tape everything. **— Socrates**

An unidentified **farrier** in **Memphis, Tennessee,** rebuilds horse's hooves with the help of duct tape: after creating a duct tape shell around the damaged equine foot, he pours in "hoof cement" and lets it set.

We've found that wrapping feet in duct tape to begin with helps prevent damage. We're not sure about horses, but Tim's tennis shoes have lasted almost fourteen years now.

Fathers and teachers, I ponder: "what is hell?" I maintain that it is the suffering of being unable to find your duct tape. — **Dostoevsky**

Physical therapist **R.H.** has found plenty of uses for duct tape in **Roseville, Minnesota.** He places a strip on patients' backs to remind them to maintain a neutral-position posture while performing daily activities. He also suggests wrapping ankles with duct tape immediately after a sprain—it provides stability and helps reduce swelling.

We like to duct tape our ankles every day to avoid spraining them in the first place.

8

T.P. in **Happy Jack, Arizona,** chops a lot of firewood. To get the most out of a tree, he secures small limbs and twigs together with duct tape and makes bundles for the wood stove.

Hey, T.P., if you tape branches to yourself, it's easier to sneak up on unsuspecting trees.

Spare the duct tape, spoil the job. — **Traditional**

Woodbury, Minnesota, can be proud of **R.S.** He fixed his foam beer can cooler with duct tape over ten years ago and it's still holding up proud.

We've done the same. Jim here also tapes the can holder right to his hand so he's not always losing his drink.

9

Duct tape in time saves dimes. — **B. Franklin**

THE REAL HISTORY OF DUCT TAPE

by Jim and Tim

SOCRATES DUCT
(artist's rendering)

Tim and me researched the history of duct tape extensively—we even looked in books. As far as we can figure out, duct tape was invented in Greece in about 400 B.C. by a guy named Socrates Duct. His house had a big hole in one of the walls which was letting a draft in. When Duct went out to the woods to get some wood to fix the hole, he accidentally got some pine sap stuck to the bottom of his toga, which stuck to his leg and made him really uncomfortable. When he got home, Duct ripped off the sticky strip of toga and stuck it over the hole in the wall, and just like that, no more draft!

He showed his repair job to his buddies, and they started using the combination of cloth and sticky stuff to fix all sorts of stuff. They called it Duct tape after Socrates Duct, but then he got famous and dropped the "Duct" so he only had one name like Madonna and Cher. After that, everybody started asking him what other ideas he had, and pretty soon he was spouting off about everything. The rest is history.

THE OTHER REAL HISTORY OF DUCT TAPE

Despite Jim and Tim's research, most adhesive historians prescribe to another theory of the development of duct tape. Many agree that adhesive tape was invented in the 1920s by 3M company researchers led by Richard Drew.

During World War II, the American armed forces needed a strong, waterproof mending material that could be ripped by hand and used to make quick repairs to jeeps, aircraft, and other military equipment. The tape also had to keep moisture out of ammunition boxes. The Johnson and Johnson company's Permacel division, which had by then developed its own line of adhesive tapes, helped the war effort by combining cloth mesh (which rips easily) with a rubber-based adhesive, and then gave that combination a rubberized, waterproof coating. **11**

Following the war, housing in the United States boomed, and many new homes featured forced-air heating and air-conditioning units that relied on duct work to distribute warmth and coolness. Johnson and Johnson's strong military tape made the perfect material for binding and repairing the duct work. By changing the color of the tape's rubberized top coat to sheet metal gray, "duct" tape was born.

"You know what, Tim? I like our story better."
"Me too, Jim. No duct tape before World War II. I'm so sure!"
"Yeah. Right."

Over one hundred canoe enthusiasts from throughout North America have shared their duct tape canoe-repair stories with Jim and Tim. They call it the "Canoeists' Companion" and say a strip on both the inside and outside of a hole will hold for an entire

12

season (some suggest adding previously-chewed bubble gum between layers to help stop leaks). Among the more resourceful paddlers is **T.M.** of **Camp Keive, Maine.** T. and his companions once wrapped their canoe around a rock in heavy rapids, and the boat ended up resembling a banana. Duct tape repaired a broken seat and a huge rip right at the waterline, and the canoeists were able to paddle the banana boat four miles to the nearest ranger station.

I duct tape, therefore I am. **— Jim**

In **White Bear Lake, Minnesota, Andrew** and his video production associates stuck a ball of used gaff tape (black duct tape used by the entertainment industry) to the hood of their van and wagered on how long it would stay there. When they returned home twenty miles later, the tape ball remained on the hood, and Andrew won the bet.

Thanks for the idea, Andrew. We're making a duct tape ball hood ornament for the Duct Tape Truck—nothing says "high class" like a decoration made from pewter on a roll!

13

M.S. of **Crete, Illinois,** operates an aerial lift. On indoor jobs, he wraps the tires in duct tape to prevent rubber marks on tile and carpeting.

Hey, M.S., give us a call. We can use your services to help add another layer to Duct Tape World's giant ball of duct tape (largest in the world!).

Some people see broken things and say, "Trash."
I see broken things and say, "Get the duct tape." **— G.B. Shaw**

Green Bay, Wisconsin, resident **M.A.** uses duct tape for a money clip while traveling because it doesn't set off metal detectors in airport security gates, and it helps cash stick to the inside of his pocket for extra protection.

You're thinking right! Jim duct tapes quarters for emergency phone calls behind his knees—less hair to rip off!

14

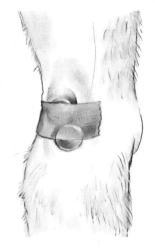

That's one small job for duct tape, one giant cost-saver for mankind.
— **N. Armstrong** (to Jim after he fixed the lunar vehicle with duct tape; see page 114).

J.H. in **Jackson, Michigan,** found an ingenious use for duct tape while working as a museum security guard. The museum sells helium balloons, which often get away from children and end up resting on the museum's thirty-foot ceiling. At night, however, changing air temperatures cause the balloons to float down, which sometimes sets off the museum's high-tech security alarm at 3 A.M. Since each false alarm costs the museum $25, J.H. had to come up with a way to retrieve the balloons. The resourceful guard covered a balloon with duct tape—sticky-side out—and attached a very long string. He then let the "sticky" balloon rise to the ceiling and attach itself to the wayward balloons, and then pulled them down. He still uses this method and sometimes retrieves twenty-five to thirty balloons a day!

15

Good one, J.H. I use the same method to get my kids' kites out of trees, and Jim uses it to get his kids out of trees.

We dream of a world where people don't think in terms of black or white, but only in shades of duct tape gray. **— Jim and Tim**

When **Katie** of **Duluth, Minnesota,** cracked the watermelon boat she was making for a party, she repaired it with duct tape.

In the future, Katie, wrap the watermelon entirely in duct tape before you start cutting. That way it will never break, and your watermelon will look like a fancy aluminum fishing boat!

In **South St. Paul, Minnesota, D.K.'s** mother uses duct tape as a safety precaution while working in a green house. She wraps her fingers with duct tape when trimming rose bushes so they don't get stabbed by the thorns.

Remember, D.K., if mom ever does get cut, duct tape and a little cotton makes an effective bandage—and duct tape alone makes a great tourniquet.

Frankly, Scarlet, I'll stick with duct tape. **— R. Butler**

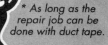
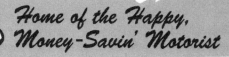

M.R. of **South Miami, Florida,** tells us that duct tape came to the rescue when Hurricane Andrew struck Miami. The storm's fury caused the sliding glass doors to detach from M.R.'s house, and wind and rain began coming in around their frames. Losing the doors would mean certain destruction to the home, so M.R. quickly applied duct tape around both doors and stopped the hurricane from entering the house. The roof blew off, but the doors held fast.

You should have duct taped the roof, M.R. Fact is, lots of folks use duct tape to prepare for hurricanes—some even call it "Hurricane Tape." When Hurricane Hugo approached the East Coast, residents used 64,104 rolls of duct tape (that's 33 million yards!) supplied by Manco. We don't live in hurricane country, but Jim does use duct tape to prepare his house when his three boys are released for summer vacation.

18

Walk softly and carry a big roll of duct tape. **— T. Roosevelt**

J.C. of **Falcon Heights, Minnesota,** opened her van door, and it came entirely out of the track. Unable to get it back together, a local duct tape pro assisted in securely taping the van door in place for the trip to the car dealer for repair. Also, when **J.B.** of **Stillwater, Minnesota,** suffered a car accident in Oregon, his mechanic duct taped the rear door shut until J.B. could get the car to a body repair shop back home. The car made it all the way back to Minnesota with the door still closed tight.

You're not the only ones! We have so much duct tape holding the doors onto our truck, they don't open anymore. We just crawl in and out through the windows.

A man is rich in proportion to the number of things he has duct taped. — **H.D. Thoreau**

In **Plymouth, Minnesota, C.I.'s** grandfather was such a duct tape aficionado that when he passed on, his family thought it only appropriate to duct tape his coffin shut. They all signed the tape as part of their farewell.

We can only hope our families do the same for us someday, C.I.

P.I., also from **Plymouth, Minnesota** (any relation to C.I.?), found his 20- and 36-foot ladders both fell short when he wanted to paint
20 his house, so he duct taped them together.

Next time, P.I., duct tape the whole house and never paint again!

The duct tape is mightier than the wood glue. — **Shakespeare**

J. and **J.K.** of **Minneapolis, Minnesota,** have a friend named Gary who once used duct tape to secure a board five feet outside of his third-story apartment so he could barbecue outdoors.

Good one, but don't try this at home, kids. If for some reason the board breaks, your downstairs neighbors might think it's raining fire and brimstone!

Duct tape can get you through times with no money better than money can get you through times with no duct tape. **— T. Anderson**

K.Z. of **Cove, Nevada,** slid off a mountain road and found herself stuck in the snow. Her husband put duct tape to the test. After taping her car's bumper to the bumper of his car, he towed her back up onto the road.

Tell your husband we say "good job," K.Z. Keep a roll in the car at all times—you can always count on it to see you through.

A.N. works as a recreational director in a **Waco, Texas,** children's home. Using discarded cardboard appliance and furniture boxes and a roll of duct tape, she created a maze for two hundred kids to crawl through. Duct tape turned out to be the only adhesive strong enough to withstand the maze's heavy traffic.

Wrap the kids' knees with duct tape to prevent premature pant wear-through—that's what we do, and Tim's been wearing the same jeans for almost twenty years now.

Most people duct tape where the problem is.
I try to duct tape where the problem will be. — **W. Gretzky**

A **Superior, Wisconsin,** family didn't let an injured finger spoil their vacation. After "Mom" damaged a digit on a water slide, "Dad" used two popsicle sticks and a strip of duct tape to splint the finger in place. Mom kept the splint on throughout their holiday and her finger healed fine.

Tim and I find that a strip or two behind each thigh also helps avoid that annoying "gripping" when you hit a dry patch on the water slide.

Duct tape is dead. — **Nietzsche**   Nietzsche is dead — **Jim and Tim**

K.C., who works at **Denver, Colorado's** Museum of Natural History, reports that duct tape is used to keep dinosaur bones in place while staff members prepare the steel armatures that hold the bones together.

It was the lack of duct tape during the Mesozoic period that led to the dinosaurs' demise—if they had duct tape to cover those tar pits, we'd be snacking on McBronto burgers today!

E.V. of the **Miss American Queen Beauty Pageant** isn't the only duct tape fan to pass along this hint: Some beauty pageant contestants, including Miss America hopefuls, find that a few well-placed strips of duct tape can save money and trips to the plastic surgeon. The upper half of many contestants' torsos defy gravity with the help of duct tape, particularly during the evening gown and swimsuit portions of the contest.

*Readers of our first book, **The Duct Tape Book**, will remember that by using tip #40, duct tape can also help with face lifts! Hey, another name for duct tape— "Plastic Surgeon on a Roll!"*

If there is a better way to do it, it probably involves duct tape. **— T. A. Edison**

F.P. of **Parker, Colorado,** likes to wrap his socks in duct tape from his ankles to his pant legs. When hiking, the tape keeps cockleburs off his socks; on the ski trail, it keeps the snow from caking on.

Keep wrapping, F.P.—an eight-ply coating of duct tape around your lower half might help make you impervious to snake bite.

While fishing near Galveston, Texas, **P.B. Jr.** of **Oklahoma City, Oklahoma,** came across a wounded twenty-pound red fish. The fish's dorsal fin was torn so badly it could only roll over on its back and travel in circles when it tried to swim. Using duct tape from the roll he always carries in his tackle box, P.B. reinforced the fin, and the fish swam off with ease.

Another fish story? We don't think so. Just another life-saving miracle performed with the all-powerful adhesive.

Take away my people but leave my factories, and soon grass will grow on the factory floors. Take away my factories but leave my people, and soon we will have a new and better factory! Take away my duct tape, and all hell will break loose. — **A. Carnegie**

M.B. of **Abrams, Wisconsin,** reports that he got a dollar bill stuck in the bill changer of a pop machine. To rescue the bill, he fed a strip of duct tape into the changer rollers. The duct tape stuck to the bill and he was able to rescue his dollar from the clutches of the machine.

You are truly a duct tape visionary! Tim and I have believed for a long time that duct tape will eventually replace paper money. After all, duct tape has much more value than paper.

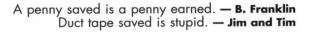

A penny saved is a penny earned. — **B. Franklin**
Duct tape saved is stupid. — **Jim and Tim**

Wheatland, Wyoming's C.B. loves to wrap gifts in duct tape. "I never use paper," she says. "Duct tape comes in perfect colors for all occasions, it doesn't rip open, and I never have to put a tag on packages because my friends and family always know who sent them the one wrapped in duct tape."

*We do the same, C.B. It's the perfect wrapping for the gift that says, "Open me **eventually**."*

28 Veterinarians across the country share a fondness for duct tape. Some D.V.M.s report using it to hold dogs' split toenails together while waiting for the adhesive to set. **A.P.**, a vet in **Kiowa, Colorado,** puts duct tape over vet wrap after sweating a horse's legs. It's the only thing the doc has found that keeps the wrap from slipping and sliding.

*Great tips! Of course, if you want to save money on vet bills, try tip #57 from our first book, **The Duct Tape Book**.*

A life without duct tape is not worth living. — **Plato**

In **Englewood, Colorado, T.O.** cures warts with duct tape by following this procedure:

1. Wrap wart in duct tape.
2. Let stand six or seven days.
3. Remove duct tape.

The wart should be gone.

Duct tape helps us get rid of all sorts of annoyances. Once Jim taped the receiver to the phone and didn't have to talk to a telemarketer for two weeks.

Careful: this method may work on more than just warts!

Knowledge is power. Power is duct tape. Therefore, duct tape is knowledge. — **F. Bacon**

T.N. of **St. Paul, Minnesota,** seals his kids' lunch bags with a strip of duct tape every day. It helps his children quickly identify the plain brown bag as theirs, keeps the contents inside, and acts as the family's secret way of saying, "I love you. Have a good day."

We have nothing to add to that beautiful story. I can't think of anything more that needs saying, and Jim's eyes are welled up with tears. God bless us, everyone!

The glow of one roll of duct tape is to me worth more than money. — **T. Jefferson**

To avoid losing loose change, **J.T.** in **Milwaukee, Wisconsin,** uses duct tape to line the inside of her old, beat-up purses.

Remember, you can also just duct tape loose change and other belongings to your body, and you won't need to carry that purse.

While waiting to board an airplane in San Pedro Sula, Honduras, **S.G.** of **Avon Lake, Ohio,** and his fellow travelers were delayed because a vulture ripped a hole in the plane's wing, delaying takeoff. S.G. produced his trusty traveling companion—a roll of duct tape—and the pilots used it to repair the wing. After the crew thoroughly tested the wing, passengers boarded and the plane successfully made the one-hour flight over the mountains to Guatemala City.

31

You must be proud, S.G. We're certain duct tape has helped NASA meet launch times on more than one occasion—is it any wonder we call it the ultimate power tool?

Sometimes a roll of duct tape is just a roll of duct tape. — **S. Freud**

When he washes his car in the winter, **C.M.** of **Medina, Ohio,** covers the door keyholes with duct tape to prevent water from getting in and freezing his locks shut.

Clever, C.M., but if you cover your entire car in duct tape like us Duct Tape Pros, you would never even have to wash the car—just retape whenever you want that just-out-of-the-showroom look. And duct tape never rusts!

32 **Bark River, Michigan's, D.S.** wraps old softballs in duct tape before giving them to the dog to play with. With its protective coating, the insides of the ball stay inside, and D.S. doesn't have to pick up all that softball string.

We do the same thing, D.S. Not only does it save work, but it helps clean the dogs' teeth and keeps their breath duct tape fresh! (But hey, come on. Bark River? Who you trying to kid?)

All we are is duct tape in the wind. — **Socrates**

When his iguana lost its tail, **R.S.** in **Roseville, Minnesota,** put it back on with a popsicle-stick-and-duct-tape splint. The tail—and the iguana—healed up fine.

Nice job, R.S., but don't amphibians' tails grow back by themselves? We know that doesn't work with mammals. Tim's dog taught us a hard lesson there. Fortunately, we were able to fashion a duct tape tail replacement, and now he doesn't tip over nearly as much.

Duct tape your own stuff, no matter what people say. — **Karl Marx**

It's safety first for **D.F.** of **Omama, Arkansas**. To avoid slipping on ice while doing farm chores in the winter, she punched small tacks through strips of duct tape and fastened the "studded" tape to the bottom of her shoes with more duct tape. "It works great!" she says.

That's a great idea for golfers, too, D.F. No more goofy looking two-tone shoes with that flap thing over the front. Just use D.F.'s plan on your favorite tennies. If you like that flap thing, just add another strip!

34

Bradenton, Florida's E.K. used to have all sorts of trouble locating her car in large shopping center parking lots. After attaching a big red duct tape flower to her car's antenna, however, she no longer wanders aimlessly on large patches of asphalt.

Thanks, E.K., for a shining example of how the introduction of colored duct tape has enhanced our society's quality of life.

Duct tape it now or pay the repair guy later. — **Jim and Tim**

A.A. of **Hollywood, South Carolina,** keeps duct tape nearby when catching small alligators—strips off the great gray roll help him keep the 'gators' mouths shut.

Your tip came to us just in time, A.A. We had to use it on our tour, and it worked great, even on some of the big guys (see page 79).

When his family reunion was threatened by the lack of a volleyball **36** net, **J.B.** of **Natrona Heights, Pennsylvania,** came to the rescue by fashioning one from his ever-handy roll of duct tape.

We also use it to mark once and for all those ever-changing in-bounds lines. Works with all sorts of other games, too—duct tape is like having a sporting goods store on a roll.

If a man does not keep pace with his companions, perhaps it is because he has stopped to fix something with duct tape. — **H.D. Thoreau**

When he goes whitewater rafting, **Charleston, West Virginia's J.G.** keeps his eyeglasses on his face with a duct tape strap—he says it holds better than those available in stores!

And remember, J.G., if you ever break your frames and find yourself in too big of a hurry to fix them with duct tape, just tape the lenses to your face.

To err is human. To repair with duct tape, divine. **— Shakespeare**

J.N. of **Shoreview, Minnesota,** had some trouble with his car's windshield washers: they shot the cleaner fluid over the roof and missed the windshield. Using a few strips of duct tape, J.N. fashioned "hoods" over both washers, directing the fluid where it was needed—on the windshield.

We ran out of washer stuff once, so we just covered the Duct Tape Truck's windshield with duct tape to keep it clean. Sadly, some highway patrolman have no appreciation for duct tape.

38 Both **L.H.** in **Talladega, Alabama,** and **K.M.** of **Lake Charles, Louisiana,** use duct tape to help them chaperone high school students. To make sure students stay in their hotel rooms after curfew, the chaperones adhere a strip of duct tape between each room's door frame and door. The students stay in their rooms because they know any duct tape that has moved is a dead giveaway of late night escapades.

Thanks for the idea. With this new method Jim can stop taping his kids to their beds.

Duct tape it today, keep the plumber away. — **Traditional**

When **S.B.** of **Sierra Vista, Arizona,** discovered he had forgotten his tent ropes, he salvaged his camping trip by fashioning replacement cords with duct tape.

S.B. knows the one simple truth about outdoor living: never—ever—go camping without a roll of the Camper's Companion in your backpack. Never!

Duct tape helps **M.M.** in **Dublin, California,** repair rips in her plastic garment bags.

With duct tape and a garbage bag, you can fashion your own rip-proof garment bag in a variety of lovely designer colors.

Ask not what your country can duct tape for you, but what you can duct tape for your country. **— J.F.K.**

D.R., a sandblaster in **New London, Iowa,** uses duct tape as "masking tape" to cover whatever he doesn't want to blast.

Fighting abrasive sands with duct tape is nothing new to us, D.R. Jim's family was able to trek through the Oklahoma dust bowl in the 1930s thanks to Grandpa's idea of covering everyone's face with duct tape. They were on their way to find work in California. When the dust cleared, however, they found themselves in Wisconsin.

40

Men are not prisoners of fate, but only prisoners of their lack of duct tape. — **F.D.R.**

Many readers of Jim and Tim's first book, *The Duct Tape Book*, suggest covering the bottom of table and chair legs with duct tape to prevent scratching floors.

Good idea, but a little shortsighted. We recommend covering your entire floor in duct tape. Not only will you never scratch it, but you never have to wax, and you can always replace the tape when it gets really dirty.

In his former job with the United States Food and Drug Administration, **S.D.** of **Berlin, Wisconsin,** carried a roll of duct tape with him as he inspected food processing plants. He used duct tape strips to collect filth and other evidence of poor sanitation for his reports. With the duct-tape-enhanced visual aids, sanitary problems he discovered received immediate attention.

Once again, duct tape is the unsung hero in our nation's fight against infectious bacteria. We're all proud of you, S.D.

This is the tape that mends men's soles. — **T. Payne**

After fixing his broken fishing rod with duct tape, **M.D.** of **San Francisco, California,** caught a six-pound rainbow trout in the Santa Cruz Mountains.

Good job, M.D. And remember, as long as there's a roll of duct tape in your tackle box, you're never out of bait.

During the holidays, **C.L.** of **New Richmond, Wisconsin,** uses the leftover cardboard from used rolls of duct tape to make candle holders for wide-based candles, and with a little red and green duct tape she fashions holly to give gifts that Christmas cheer.

Try using new rolls, C.L., and give your loved ones two gifts in one—and something they can use all year long!

One thing only I know, and that is that I know duct tape. — **Socrates**

M.W. of **Mankato, Minnesota,** picks up extra cash passing out free samples at the grocery store. To relieve foot discomfort during long, six-hour shifts, she duct tapes sponges to the bottom of her shoes.

We've found this same application turns the drudgery of cleaning floors into fun work and healthy exercise.

After his neighbor fell off the roof and injured a leg, **Bettendorf, Iowa's D.M.** used duct tape and two two-by-fours to fashion an emergency splint.

43

Nice job, D.M., and let this incident be a warning to us all: If you plan on spending any amount of time on your roof, by all means take precautions and duct tape yourself to the chimney or something.

A repair job duct taped is a repair job done. **— Traditional**

A little boy in **Colorado** accidentally dropped his turtle while running in the street. The shell cracked and the local vet said the turtle could not be saved—it would have to be put to sleep. The boy and his family didn't accept the doctor's advice; they took the turtle home, and carefully put its shell back together with duct tape. The shell eventually mended, and the turtle lives on!

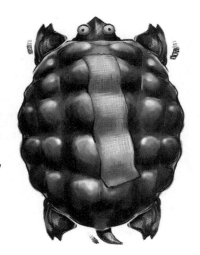

44

Another life saved with duct tape. Is it any wonder four out of five dentists recommend using it to hold those little spit bibs in place?

The quality of a person's life is in direct proportion to their commitment to excellence, and their use of duct tape. — **V. Lombardi**

PUBLIC SERVICE ANNOUNCEMENT

TIM: If you've read all the real stories so far, you probably noticed that duct tape now comes in a variety of colors.

JIM: That's right, Tim. Red, yellow, brown, green, blue, black, white—the list goes on!

TIM: This recent advance opens up a whole new world of duct taping possibilities!

JIM: Like green for mini-golf turf repair.

TIM: Or yellow to create fake center lines on the highway.

JIM: Right. And don't forget Naugahyde™ brown for comfy chair repair! And, hey, maybe they could use blue to fix that hole in the ozone layer!

TIM: Good idea, Jim! There's also designer black—perfect for mending the rip in your tuxedo. And red—to fix your red stuff.

JIM: We all have red stuff that needs repair! Go out and buy some colored duct tape today!

This has been a public service announcement from Jim and Tim, The Duct Tape Guys.™

"You know what, Tim? I still like the traditional silver-gray best."
"Me too, Jim. I guess there's no stopping progress, though."

South Pole explorer **Norman Vaughan**, after whom Admiral Byrd named Antarctica's Mount Vaughan, says that during ice-cap explorations, he keeps his roll of duct tape next to him in his sleeping bag. Arctic temperatures prevent the adhesive from working well, and body heat keeps the tape warm! He and his fellow explorers call duct tape "1,000-mile tape" because the duct tape they use to line the runners of their sleds (to make them more slippery) lasts for about 1,000 miles.

Jim and I covered our pickup truck with duct tape to make it more aerodynamic. Now we get two more miles per gallon—I think we'll call it "two-more-miles-per-gallon" tape.

46

In order to both make a fashion statement and publicize her love of duct tape, self-proclaimed Duct Tape Girl **C.B.** in **Grafton**, **Massachusetts**, fashioned an entire purse out of duct tape.

Not only fashionable, but sensible, too, Duct Tape Girl: Duct tape gray goes with everything.

Duct tape is the only tool you need in your toolbox. **— Jim and Tim**

Back in the mid-1980s, **T.W.** of **Lakeville, Minnesota,** attended college Halloween parties at the University of Minnesota-Duluth dressed as "Duct Tape Man." He covered his clothes in duct tape, fashioned a mask and cape from the silver wonder roll, and stuck a big duct tape "D" to his chest. By the end of the evening, Duct Tape Man had done his duty, and every guest went home with duct tape highlighting some part of their costume.

OK, we get the mask and cape part, but what's so special about covering your clothes with duct tape?

Come on up and see me sometime.
And bring your duct tape. — **M. West**

E.C. of **Denver, Colorado,** lined his leaky gutters with duct tape, and they haven't allowed seepage since.

Parents of infants, take note: The same principle can be applied to diapers.

J. & **J.P.** of **Unionville, Indiana,** symbolically secured their marital union with wedding bands made of duct tape—the only rings they have ever exchanged!

Duct tape is designed to create a strong bond—what could be a more appropriate symbol of marriage?

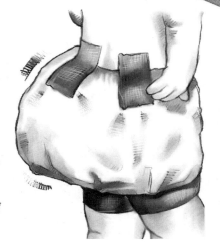

48

All we need is duct tape. Duct tape is all we need. — **Lennon/McCartney**

Before hitting the slopes, **T.B.** of **Brooklyn Center, Minnesota,** places random strips of duct tape on his new skis—that way, he theorizes, thieves will think they're damaged and won't steal them.

Really? We would have thought the glint of duct tape would catch a thief's eye—after all, it increases the value of anything it's on!

After his four-wheel-drive truck broke a tie-rod in the middle of the woods, **W.T.**, a **Northern Minnesota** trapper used wire and duct tape to hold his drive train together. He was able to drive out to the nearest road to wait for a tow to the repair shop.

Why take it to the shop? Sounds like you did all the repairing you needed to, W.T. Heck, we've replaced nearly every moving part on the Duct Tape Truck with duct tape. Rides pretty smooth, but cornering gets tricky.

When the going gets tough,
the tough pull out their roll of duct tape. **— Traditional**

Writing on the Infobahn, **"DEZERT"** reports that he uses duct tape to weatherstrip and cover rat holes in his cabin on the **Utah** outback. He credits the reluctance of rats to chew through duct tape to its bad flavor and stickiness.

On the contrary, Dezert. Duct tape tastes great and helps keep your tacos together. Must just be a really good job of taping.

Cabby **G.H.** of **Seattle, Washington,** was prone to accidents, and his seat belt wouldn't fasten, so he fixed the buckle with duct tape. Upon hitting a street cleaner while traveling in excess of forty-five miles an hour, the duct tape reinforced seat belt held fast and G.H. was unharmed!

We're glad to hear you're safe, G.H., but be careful—as far as safety features are concerned, it's best to stay with original equipment. We learned the hard way with the air bag Jim made for the Duct Tape Truck. After a recent fender bender, paramedics had to use the Jaws of Life to pry Jim's face off of the steering wheel. I warned him, "Sticky-side in!"

If my doctor told me I only had six minutes to live, I wouldn't brood.
I'd duct tape a little faster. — **I. Asimov**

L.C. of **Thorofare, New Jersey,** repairs upholstery rips with duct tape patches cut into the shapes of flowers and stars.

If you had covered all your furniture with duct tape as soon as you brought it home, it would never have worn thin in the first place.

P.G. of **Sturgeon Bay, Wisconsin,** covered his family's entire swing set with duct tape to prevent rust and as a safety measure for the kids.

We like to cover the kids in duct tape. That way they're safe everywhere—and won't rust!

Success is more a function of consistent use of duct tape than it is of genius. — **A. Wang**

G.C. of **Point Blank, Texas,** uses a strip of duct tape to seal the space between his stove and countertop—it keep things from falling in the gap.

Hey, great tape-saving idea, G.C.—we've just been taping everything to the counter.

S.A. enjoys a pleasant soak in her bathtub in **Superior, Wisconsin,** by sealing the overflow drain with duct tape to get in a few extra inches of water.

If you're looking for a real bath, S.A., try Tim's method: tape the shower curtain tightly to the wall for a full-body, stand-up soak.

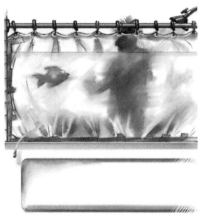

Genius dazzles mortals' eyes. It is only duct tape in disguise. — **Anonymous**

It only takes four strips of duct tape for **M.J.V.** in **Sarasota Springs, Florida,** to make sidewalk tic-tac-toe games for his kids. A few more strips reinforces the cardboard Xs and Os.

Sounds like a challenge, M.J.V.—we'll take the upper-left corner to start.

Day care provider **D.G.** of **Ruby, New York,** entertains the kids by combining duct tape and cardboard boxes to create giant dinosaurs, houses, buildings, ticket booths, and pirate ships.

Call us if you ever need work, D.G. The expansion of Duct Tape World starts soon.

L. and **T. S.** of **San Diego, California,** get extra mileage out of their birthday party pinatas by duct taping them back together.

Who needs pinatas? Duct tape the candy to your ceiling and just try to get it down—no blindfolds needed!

All progress springs from duct tape. **— B. Franklin**

ORGANICALLY GROWN DUCT TAPE?

Randall Ripley, Dean of the College at Ohio State University, sent Jim and Tim the following letter:

Dear Jim and Tim:

In your first book, you failed to mention anything about organically grown duct tape as developed during the Eisenhower administation. I once owned a government publication about growing duct tape, an unimaginatively titled treatise called "Duct Tape Horticulture" which the U.S. Department of Agriculture published in 1957. Unfortunately, I lost my copy in a move. You may be able to find it in the Library of Congress.

According to the publication, as I recall, both President Eisenhower and his secretary of agriculture, Ezra Taft Benson, were proponents of organic duct tape. Alarmingly, most historical data concerning the Eisenhower administration as well as biographies of Ike fail to mention his fondness for America's favorite adhesive. The only exception I know of is Stephen Ambrose's discussion of the importance of duct tape in securing the Normandy beaches on D-Day—a use attributed directly to Eisenhower as Supreme Commander.

Sincerely,

Randall Ripley

The true leader always has duct tape. — **Carl Jung**

Thanks, Dean Ripley, for letting us know about this important aspect of American history (and we call ourselves Duct Tape Pros). We did track down the pamphlet, but only the cover was intact. The text had been purposely obscured. Since we were at the library, we read through the Warren Commission Report and discovered that witnesses claim seeing a strip of duct tape stuck to the fence near the grassy knoll. Not only that, but Kennedy breathed air that came through ducts, and Lincoln enjoyed feeding ducks on the White House lawn. Coincidence? We thought so, but then we remembered you said most historians ignore Eisenhower's duct tape connection. We're developing a conspiracy theory and plan to send it to Oliver Stone. Keep in touch.

Duct Tape
Horticulture

©1957
U.S. Government
Document Office
Doument #03-52JK-DT06-70

Life is an adventure in duct taping. — **N. Cousins**

When **K.G.** and his colleagues in **Wheat Ridge, Colorado,** remove asbestos, they keep their baggy, disposable suits in place with temporary belts made by folding duct tape in half lengthwise.

The great irony of the heating and cooling industry is that those same visionaries who helped give us duct tape were shortsighted with their widespread use of cancer-causing asbestos. Had they known then what they know now, they could have used special fire-retardant duct tape in its place. We live, we learn, and duct tape helps hold the lessons of life together.

56

Midland, Texas', M.A. was just one of the many Americans who reported using duct tape to repair rips in vacuum cleaner bags.

And remember, if you run out of vacuum cleaner bags, wrap your feet in duct tape sticky-side out and simply "walk up" the dust and dirt from your carpets.

Duct tape is never expensive, it is PRICELESS. — **Tim**

Radio personality **P.L.** of **Woodbury, Minnesota,** swears that after losing her poultry pins one Thanksgiving, she used duct tape to seal the turkey's skin and hold the stuffing in.

Sounds tasty, P.L. And don't forget: duct tape has a considerably lower fat content than turkey skin. By the way, careful readers may have

noticed that the majority of these real stories come from Minnesotans like P.L. Is it any wonder so many people call duct tape "Minnesota Chrome?"

Sun Prairie, Wisconsin's S.S. uses duct tape to replace the webbing in his lawn chairs after the original straps wear out.

*Why wait? Reinforce new chairs with duct tape to match your easy-to-clean, duct tape covered picnic table—**The Duct Tape Book,** hint #152.*

The expectations of life depend upon duct tape. The mechanic that would perfect his work must first find his duct tape. — **Chinese Proverb**

Annoyed by the lack of grommets to hold tubes of caulk and glue to her workshop pegboard, **B.S.** in **Old Hickory, Tennessee,** started making her own. She just tapes a duct tape tab on the tube and then punches a hole in the tab.

*OK, but if you've got duct tape in the first place, what the heck do you need caulk and glue for? (And, hey, that grommet tip is right out of our first book, **The Duct Tape Book,** hint #112. Remember, everyone you know needs a copy.)*

58

In **Happy Jack, Arizona, T.P.** bundles old newspapers for recycling using duct tape.

Those bundles make wonderful building material, too, T.P. We plan to use them to help complete the construction of the Duct Tape World expansion under budget!

It is high time the ideal of success should be replaced with the ideal of duct tape. — **A. Einstein**

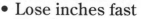

Instead of wasting money on a luggage rack, **D.P.** of **Jax, Florida**, says his father-in-law secured luggage to the top of his car with duct tape. It held tight on a two-day drive along the interstate.

We use the same method to hold the Duct Tape Pro Camper on the Duct Tape Truck. Actually, the camper itself is pretty much just a bunch of duct tape around some old refrigerator boxes.

NASA sends a roll of duct tape on every mission. In fact, on the ill-fated **Apollo 13** flight, duct tape saved our astronauts by allowing them to modify a command module CO_2 filter to fit the lunar escape module which was acting as their lifeboat during their crippled return to Earth. Without duct tape, the astronauts would have died from their own exhalation.

We've been doing secret work with NASA for years. I guess now that Univeral Studios has revealed the duct tape/NASA connection, we can openly admit our participation in the space program.

The mind, once expanded with the knowledge of duct tape, never returns to its original size. — **O.W. Holmes**

The **M.P.** family of **Cape Coral, Florida,** uses duct tape to create "roads" and "buildings" on the driveway so the kids can ride their trikes through their own little town.

We like to duct tape cardboard boxes to the driveway for three-dimensional buildings—that way the kids can also play "Godzilla."

When **Shoreview, Minnesota's, C.B.** checks disposable diapers and finds them dry, the happy parent reseals them with duct tape.

Great idea. Cloth diaper users can use duct tape instead of safety pins to prevent pin jabs.

It makes a big step in man's development when he comes to realize
that duct tape can be called in to help him do a better job
than he can do alone. **— A. Carnegie**

When **T.D.** of **Roseau, Minnesota,** couldn't find rope or bungie cords to secure his load to the top of his truck, he used duct tape.

Duct tape can also make an excellent waterproof pickup bed cover. Simply tape over the entire bed, overlapping strips of duct tape.

Nothing in the world can take the place of duct tape.
Talent will not... Genius will not... Education will not...
Duct tape alone is omnipotent. — **C. Coolidge**

Aunt Dinah's
DUCT TAPE DINER

Aunt Dinah's Duct Tape Diner
has been awarded
The Good Duct Taping Seal of Approval!

*"All my food is served on 100% Duct Tape Lined Paper Plates
and YOU Can Keep the Plate!" – Dinah*

Ask about our gray plate special!
AUNT DINAH'S DUCT TAPE DINER
Located within driving distance from anywhere in North America!

J.W. owns a racing tire company in **Brooklyn, Michigan.** He uses duct tape to secure wheel weights to racing mag wheels.

Guess that's just one reason car racers call it "200-Mile-an-Hour Tape." We turned the Duct Tape Truck's wheels into custom mags with a roll or two.

T.S. considers duct tape a photographer's most valuable tool. The **Howell, New Jersey,** shutterbug has used it to make giant spider webs and countless other props for his pictures.

Erik, the Tape the World—World Tour's official photographer, used seventeen cases of duct tape on the tour. In the rain forest he used it to make a waterproof canopy for his tripod. When the locals saw how his contraption repelled the rain, they started worshipping him. Then some sales rep showed up with a soft-serve ice cream machine and they forgot all about Erik.

The drip stops here. **— H. Truman** (referring to a duct tape faucet repair job)

A strip of duct tape wrapped securely around his pant leg is all **J.N.** of **Shoreview, Minnesota,** needs to help keep his cuff out of his bicycle chain.

Always keep a roll with you on the road. Duct tape works on ripped seats, bare handlebars, and—if used correctly—can help patch tires!

G.L., a contractor in **Lansing, Michigan,** employs a few strips of duct tape to hold blue prints to the wall at job sites.

Contractors like G.L. can save tons of time, money, and mess by using duct tape to finish drywall—no sanding, no painting, and it washes up better than wallpaper!

Keep your eyes on the stars and keep your feet on the ground and a roll of duct tape by your side. **— T. Roosevelt**

DUCT TAPE CHANGES LIVES!

| ***Tim Before*** | ***Tim After*** | ***Jim Before*** | ***Jim After*** |

Duct tape has dramatically changed my life. I'm ashamed to admit it, but I grew up using electrical tape. When Jim introduced me to duct tape, I not only discovered an easier-to-rip tape, I also found a stronger tape that was actually four rolls in one (if you rip it length-wise in strips as wide as electrical tape). I went from nerd to Duct Tape Pro almost overnight, gaining the respect of everyone around me. My wife and kids weren't ashamed to be seen with me anymore; my fellow workers started asking me for advice. I slept better and felt better.

Thanks, Jim. Thanks, duct tape. – Tim

I've always used duct tape. My parents used it to hold my diapers on. So, really, duct tape hasn't *changed* my life. Because of duct tape, my quality of life has always been good. However, when we wrote the first book, things started to change. Before *The Duct Tape Book's* success, we lived in a double-wide mobile home. Now that the money is starting to roll in, we're talkin' triple-wide. It's just a dream, but heck, if the book keeps selling, we could even go for a triple-high! Naturally, we'll use plenty of duct tape to hold it together.

Thanks to everyone who bought a book. – Jim

Editor's note: Jim's dreams came true. The photo above shows Jim atop his new triple-wide, quad-high mobile home. Notice the "penthouse master suite" on the top level, complete with patio.

PUBLIC SERVICE ANNOUNCEMENT

TIM: Jim and me discovered a bogus product.

JIM: That's right, Tim. We were watching some home shopping cable thing and saw one of those infomercials about a product called "Duct Tape in a Can."

TIM: Ya, right! Duct Tape does NOT come in a can. It comes on a roll.

JIM: If it doesn't come on a roll, it isn't tape! If it isn't tape, it can't be **Duct Tape.** Duct tape does not come in aerosol cans!

TIM: And we will not endorse its use on anything.

JIM: Right! Especially not ducts!

TIM: So when it comes to "Duct Tape in a Can," just say NO!

**This has been a public service announcement
from Jim and Tim, The Duct Tape Guys.™**

"Boy, am I ever glad we put a stop to that, Tim."

"Me too, Jim. I feel much better now."

"Me too. Well… Now what?

"I dunno. Let's go duct tape something."

TIM: Like the song says, "What the world needs now, is duct tape, sweet duct tape."

JIM: That's right! So Tim and me went off on a 367-day, 49-nation tour of the world to fix famous broken stuff.

TIM: Using only our keen duct taping abilities and the Ultimate Power Tool™, we taped the world. Our official photographer, Erik, took lots of pictures on our trip. Turn down the lights, Jim.

JIM: It's a book, Tim.

TIM: Oh, ya. Well, enjoy the pictures!

We started with Venus by Milo.
Jim thought it was busted.
I thought Milo ran out of rock.
Anyway, the hardest part of this
job was finding the right
size mannequin arm.

The Alamo takes on a silvery new look and the Duct Tape Pros save another piece of history from the powers of erosion. Think of it as cloth-embedded vinyl siding,

How did you get up there, Tim?

(before)
A job this big requires careful planning.

Jim's years of experience allow him to
quickly and easily pinpoint the damage.

(after) Pretty good job, eh?
Next year we're putting a dome over the top.
Note: We did use a few other materials on this project,
but the restoration is 95% duct tape.

They forgot to finish the Eiffel Tower, so we did. With the new duct tape walls, they can start adding office space.

(When you're a Duct Tape Pro, sometimes it's hard to be humble.)

NASA frequently asks us to help with the shuttle
program—but that's all we're allowed to tell you.
(The shuttle isn't really landing on our truck,
it's just an optical illusion.)

This wooden statue in Fiji needed a little support, so Jim made her a duct tape bikini top.

I'm relaxing for a while thinking about making duct tape dreadlocks for the guy on the right.

The little picture shows how puny this Croatian guy's hat was before we improved it with duct tape.

After Erik took this photo the Croatian guy decked Jim for putting his arm around his wife.

Ingrate.

'Gator taping in the Everglades. Jim better be careful or the next book might be by "and Tim."

We couldn't convince our host to use a fork, so we showed him how duct taping chopsticks to your fingers can really be a big help when speed eating.

Here we are restoring the actual covered wagon used by Tim's family back in the 1800s. The duct tape coating will reflect the sun and make traveling a whole lot cooler!

Left: Duct Tape bikini briefs help make David's privates less public.

Hey, Tim. Look, You have plumber butt!

Right: Jim cares for some doo-hickeys on the Notre Dame Cathedral.

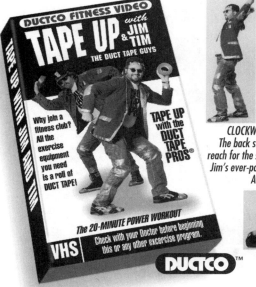

After we fixed this statue of a lady with wings and a fancy stick in Germany, a local artist said she might make a statue of us with wings and a fancy stick. We figure she can call it, "Duct Tape Guys with Wings and a Fancy Stick."

Another Greek Tragedy: This beautiful building lays in ruins because they didn't apply duct tape in time.

We thought about this
one for about an hour,
but then we decided
to move on.

(Not that duct tape
couldn't handle it.)

A sudden gust of wind set us back a couple hours in Holland.

I tell ya, though, nothing gets the adrenaline flowin' like an early morning windmill ride.

Here we are in the Hong Kong harbor making boats watertight. We also had to duct tape the oar guy's hat to scare the seagulls away.

(Shortly after we took this picture, our truck rolled off the dock into the water.)

Luckily we were on hand when the top level of this bus in Hong Kong started to fall off (hitting our truck probably didn't help).

We later deemed it safe (and pretty cool!).

Local authorities thanked us and then suggested that next time we visit Hong Kong, we should leave our truck at home.

A cultural exchange: They taught us how to prepare sushi and we taught them how to prepare a duct taped sushi serving platter.

Tim showing off his artistic side and his state-of-the-art duct taping skills.

All the world's a stage and we are merely gaffers.

Jim and me would like to take this opportunity to
encourage our readers to use a travel agent whenever
you plan a world tour. We didn't and found ourselves
putting on a lot of extra miles zig zagging
back and forth. It was stupid.

We had a dream.
We had a duct tape dream.

< Before

After >

First wooden teeth and now a duct tape nose job... George's got it all!

Working on George gave us another idea, and just like that we were off to Egypt.

Opposite page: Thanks to our duct tape reinforcements, the Aoki family's paper house survived a major earthquake. They now consider us part of the family.

Below: Polarized at the Temple of the Sun Cult. Jim's fired up and ready to get taping. Tim wants to relax and catch some rays.

There's us Duct Tape Pros
repairing hail damage to the
Sydney Opera House.

Jim's dreamin'!
Hey, shut up, Tim.

Opposite page:
By doubling their length, duct tape increased the range of this South American hunter's blow gun. He was so grateful he vowed to name his firstborn son "Jimandtim."

This page:
Here we're preparing the Iwo Jima Monument in Washington, D.C. just before a big storm.

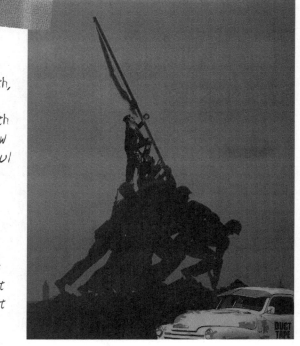

DUCT TAPE

There's Jim showing off, Just after Erik took this picture, Jim lost his balance and fell through the Ozaki's paper wall. Thank goodness for duct tape!

Here I am contemplating leaving Jim because I was getting sick of him always showing off for the Greek babes.

These old pillars in Turkey
seemed to be serving
no functional purpose,
so Jim thought up the idea
of putting a billboard
on top of them.

Good one, Jim.

If you happen to see our billboard in Turkey
and get the overwhelming urge to visit
Duct Tape World, this is what it looks like.

Behind Duct Tape World you can see part of the World's
Largest Duct Tape Ball (made by Jim and Tim).

The World's Largest Ball of (recycled)
Duct Tape! It's a gold mine!

Two down and three to go ...
The Great Pyramids are about to get Greater.

(Notice how Jim and me are starting to show
the effects of our 367-day tour?)

Tim was so absorbed in duct taping one of
the fragile stone formations in Arizona that
it took an hour before he realized I'd fallen off.

Anticipating the decline of its economy, Jim helps Russia
save money by using duct tape instead of gold leaf.

Duct tape aids in the disarmament of the former Soviet Union.
(Later we were told that this was just an antique cannon and it
wasn't even functional. Truth or diabolically clever lie?)

It's been a long and busy journey, but we feel that the world is a better place now because of our efforts and the proper application of Duct Tape.

DUCT TAPE THROUGH HISTORY

Jim and Tim feel that textbooks rarely acknowledge the role of duct tape through history. Though willing to forgive a few oversights, they felt it their duty to correct two or three of the more glaring omissions. Here are but a few of the many examples of how duct tape has helped humanity advance in the arts and sciences.

Left: *There we are helping Neil Armstrong get out of the LEM (notice the duct tape suit).*
Above: *I'm holding the flag straight while Jim repairs the Lunar Rover wheel. Unfortunately, we were mysteriously air brushed out of ALL moon landing photos!*

Just like us in the moon shot photos, our forefathers were mysteriously removed from some paintings. Here are a couple snapshots from the family album. The one on the left is of our great-grandfathers with Whistler's mother—they helped tape her upright in the chair during the lengthy studio session. On the right you see our really-great-grandpas with their neighbor Lisa. She's smiling because they just told her that Da Vinci uses duct tape to hold up his socks. Other duct tape enhanced paintings include "The Scream," whose subject was actually based on the reaction of Munch's plumber when he realized he just ran out of duct tape. Look for more of these fascinating stories about duct tape through history in future duct tape chronicles.

CEREAL

DUCT-O's ™

Breakfast of DUCT TAPE PROS

NOW YOU CAN EAT LIKE A DUCT TAPE PRO!

DUCT-O's

- They're gray!
- They look like duct tape rolls!
- They're crispy!
- They contain NO duct tape!
- Jim and Tim eat 'em!
- They're fortified!*

Ask Mom to buy some today!

*No actual nutritional value has yet been identified.

If Duct-O's are not currently available in your grocer's fine cereal section - please ask for them by name!

THE OTHER BOOKS

by Jim and Tim

Since *The Duct Tape Book* was first published, Americans have come to realize the value of compiling a great deal of useful product information into a single, convenient, and easy-to-use reference manual. Many of their readers have encouraged The Duct Tape Guys to create similar books for other products. While they haven't actually written anything yet, Jim and Tim wish to share with you their working titles as well as a brief synopsis of each book.

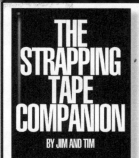

THE STRAPPING TAPE COMPANION

From super-sealing cartons to repairing a leaky sink, Jim and Tim explore the many uses of this duct tape wanna-be.

THE POST-IT™ NOTE BOOK

How the 3M Company turned a failed adhesive into the most popular notepad of all time. (But, you can stick any paper to anything with duct tape.)

HOT GLUE GUNS: The Ultimate Friendly Fire

Sure, you could use hot glue instead of duct tape, but we've never heard of anyone getting burned using duct tape.

by Jim and Tim

THE ART AND SCIENCE OF SPACKLE

Misplaced your duct tape? When it comes to repairing unsightly holes in the wall, nothing does it better than spackle.

by Jim & Tim

TWIST-TIE MANIA

They're everywhere! Those little paper- and plastic-coated wires designed to bind plastic bags. What else can you do with them? Who cares? We have duct tape!

by Jim & Tim

DO YOU PINE FOR TWINE?

This handy guide provides dozens of ideas for what to do with all of your left-over twine now that you have discovered the ultimate binding tool: duct tape.

by Jim & Tim

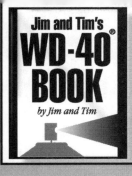

JIM AND TIM'S WD-40™ BOOK

Two simple rules to get you through life: If it doesn't move and it's supposed to, WD-40 it. If it moves and it isn't supposed to, duct tape it.

IT'S GRANDPA'S HAYWIRE HANDBOOK

Before there was duct tape, Grandpa fixed everything with Baling Wire or "Hay Wire." The "good old days" you say? We think not.

CABLE TIES: Not just for cables any more...

America's favorite method of binding unruly cables, cords, and speaker wires—they're what to reach for assuming you can't find your roll of duct tape.

PROCESSED CHEESE AND YOU.

Out of duct tape? Quick, check the 'fridge! America's favorite synthetic dairy food makes a great repair substitute.

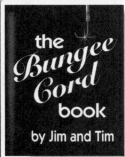

THE BUNGEE CORD BOOK

Tragically, folks who haven't discovered duct tape still secure stuff with bungee cords. Their frustration is evidenced in the high number of bungee users who jump off bridges.

WE'RE STUCK ON SUPER GLUE™

No duct tape? Here's what to do with Super Glue™ if you don't want to hang from a steel girder in a hard hat.

HOOKED ON VELCRO as told to Jim and Tim

HOOKED ON VELCRO™ AS TOLD TO JIM AND TIM

We tried to understand why people need Velcro™ when duct tape is around, but we really don't see the point.

No book. We just ate a lot of SPAM® on our World Tour.

Thanks, Hormel Foods.

—Jim and Tim

NOTES:

"Notes? Can't you think of anything else to fill this page with, Tim?"

"No. And besides, I have to go to the bathroom, Jim."

"Oh, alright. I'll cover for you. Well, that's our second book. We hope that you liked it. Remember, if you duct tape like a pro, you have to wear the right apparel. Turn the page for our Duct Tape Boutique—it has all of the fine wardrobe items that Tim and me wear during our most demanding duct taping jobs. Remember, it ain't broke, it just lacks duct tape!"